In memory of Fred.
My ginger fur-baby.
xXx

ISBN: 978-1-913339-23-4

A catalogue record of this book is available from the British Library.

MARNEY'S PUMPKIN MIX-UP

JANE RUSHMORE

SALLY DARBY

First published in the UK
2021 by Owlet Press
www.owletpress.com

Autumn had returned to the park. The leaves had fallen, and the days were getting shorter and shorter. It was time for the squirrels to gather their winter food again.

This year, children had left pumpkins around the park, giving Marney a brilliant idea . . .

"NO mix-ups this year – I'VE got a PLAN," he told the oldest squirrel.

"I'm going to get ALL the yummy seeds out of a HUGE pumpkin and hide them in a SECRET spot."

As Marney set off across the park, to the bushes where he had seen the GIANT pumpkin, he passed his friends, who were working together happily.

"Do you want to come over here and work with us?" they asked. **"No thank you,"** Marney replied quickly. **"I'm FAR too busy."** And off he went.

As Marney got closer to the pumpkin, he stumbled upon Riley the hedgehog, who was snuffling for snacks.

"Hi, Marney. What are you up to?"

"I'm going to get ALL the seeds out of the GIGANTIC pumpkin in that bush."

"Oh no, Marney," said Riley, **"don't do that, there's a—"**
"Don't worry about me." Marney laughed. **"I know what I'm doing."**

He HAD to stick to the plan – then he'd have ALL those lovely seeds. BUT, as he put his paw into the bush . . .

Marney snatched his paw back in a hurry.

"What was that?"

Pumpkins didn't USUALLY
make GROWLING noises?

Maybe SOMETHING had
made a home inside?

"I'm going to have to be a bit more careful with this one!"

thought Marney.

Meanwhile, Riley was still happily searching for snacks, with his prickly spikes keeping danger away.

This gave Marney an idea.

"Ah, those spikes are just what I need!"

he said, and he quickly scampered off to find a 'spike' of his own.

"Right . . ." said Marney,

"I'll poke that pumpkin, frighten away the creature inside, and ALL those juicy seeds will be MINE."

Marney picked up a very long stick . . .

He crept closer and closer until he could see the big orange shape, deep inside the thick bush. He carefully wriggled the stick through the tangled branches. Then gently poked the pumpkin to scare away whatever was inside.

All of a sudden . . .

"HISSSSSSSSSSSSSSSSSS!"

Yikes! Whatever this creature was,
it certainly wasn't leaving!

Marney backed away again,
but he wasn't ready to give up
on those YUMMY seeds.

He spotted a small,
dirty ball in the leaves.

He picked it up . . .

and THREW it,
as hard as he could,
at the pumpkin . . .

"MEEOOOOOOW!"

"Aargh!
This pumpkin's ALIVE!"

Marney screeched, running away as fast as his legs would carry him.

He didn't stop running until he reached
the top of the tallest tree in the park.

SQUIRREL-EATING PUMPKINS! Who knew?

As Marney looked down, he saw his friends below.

"Quick! Climb up here before that pumpkin EATS you!"

"Oh Marney," they laughed. **"That wasn't a pumpkin, it was a CAT! Didn't Riley warn you about it?"**

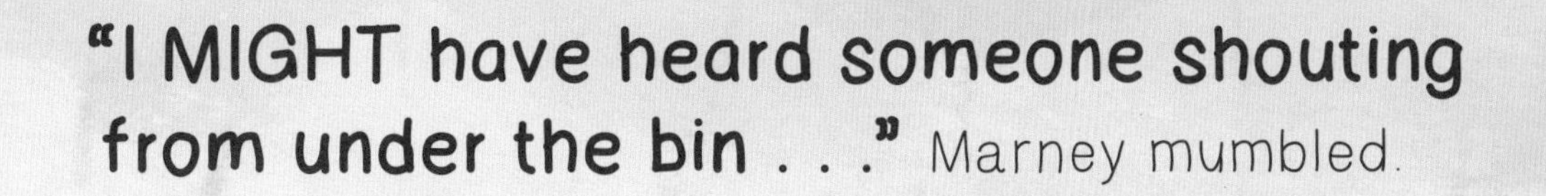

"I MIGHT have heard someone shouting from under the bin . . ." Marney mumbled.

Poor Marney . . . ANOTHER mix-up!
Maybe if he hadn't been in such a hurry,
Marney could have let Riley finish.

"We're going to work together again tomorrow," the other squirrels said. **"Will you join us?"**

And this time . . .

Marney said **"YES!"** He realised that tough jobs can be much easier when you listen to others and let them help you.

"So, did you learn anything new this year, Marney?"

asked the oldest squirrel, smiling, as he watched the squirrels working together as a team.

"Yes," Marney replied.

"I DON'T like PUMPKINS!"

MARNEY'S SPICED PUMPKIN LOAF RECIPE

YOU WILL NEED . . .

175g butter, melted
140g clear honey
1 large egg, beaten
250g pumpkin flesh, grated
100g light muscovado sugar
2 tbsp demerara sugar
350g self-raising flour
1 tbsp ground ginger
1 pinch cinnamon
1bsp orange zest

THEN THE BAKING BEGINS . . .

- Ask a grown-up to preheat the oven to 180C (160C fan /gas mark 4).
- Grease and line a loaf tin with baking paper.
- Mix the butter, honey and egg together.
- Add in the pumpkin and orange zest.
- Finally, stir in the sugar, flour and spices.
- Pour into your tin and sprinkle with the demerara sugar.
- Ask a grown-up to bake for 50-60 minutes, until golden.

Leave your loaf in the tin for 5 minutes and then tip it out onto a cooling rack.

Best enjoyed as a thick slice with some butter (and even some marmalade!)

Squirrels, foxes, badgers and birds will all enjoy your clean chopped-up pumpkin leftovers, as they can sometimes struggle to find food.